Johnny-Cake

by Joseph Jacobs

Illustrated by Emma L. Brock

G.P. Putnam's Sons   New York

E813162

COPYRIGHT, 1933, BY G. P. PUTNAM'S SONS

Eleventh Impression

J398.3
J153jo

JOHNNY-CAKE

Once upon a time there was an old man, and an old woman, and a little boy.

One morning the old woman made a Johnny-cake, and put it in the oven to bake.

"You watch the Johnny-cake while your father and I go out to work in the garden."

So the old man and the old woman went out and began to hoe potatoes, and left the little boy to tend the oven.

But he didn't watch it all the time, and all of a sudden he heard a noise, and he looked up and the oven door popped open, and out of the oven jumped Johnny-cake, and went rolling along end over end, towards the open door of the house.

The little boy ran to shut the door, but Johnny-cake was too quick for him and rolled through the door, down the steps, and out into the road long before the little boy could catch him.

The little boy ran after him as fast as he could clip it, crying out to his father and mother, who heard the uproar, and threw down their hoes and gave chase too.

But Johnny-cake outran all three a long way, and was soon out of sight, while they had to sit down, all out of breath, on a bank to rest.

On went Johnny-cake, and by-and-by he came to two well-diggers who looked up from their work and called out: "Where ye going, Johnny-cake?"

He said: "I've outrun an old man, and an old woman, and a little boy, and I can outrun you too-o-o!"

"Ye can, can ye? We'll see about that!" said they; and they threw down their picks and ran after him, but couldn't catch up with him, and soon they had to sit down by the roadside to rest.

On ran Johnny-cake, and by-and-by he came to two ditch-diggers who were digging a ditch.

"Where ye going, Johnny-cake?" said they.

He said: "I've outrun an old man, and an old woman, and a little boy, and two well-diggers, and I can outrun you too-o-o!"

"Ye can, can ye? We'll see about that!" said they; and they threw down their spades, and ran after him too. But Johnny-cake soon outstripped them also, and, seeing they could never catch him, they gave up the chase and sat down to rest.

On went Johnny-cake, and by-and-by he came to a bear. The bear said: "Where are ye going, Johnny-cake?"

He said: "I've outrun an old man, and an old woman, and a little boy, and two well-diggers, and two ditch-diggers, and I can outrun you too-o-o!"

INN OF THE
SEVEN CATS

E.L.BROCK

"Ye can, can ye?" growled the bear, "we'll see about that!" and trotted as fast as his legs could carry him after Johnny-cake, who never stopped to look behind him.

Before long the bear was left so far behind that he saw he might as well give up the hunt first as last, so he stretched himself out by the roadside to rest.

On went Johnny-cake, and by-and-by he came to a wolf. The wolf said: "Where ye going, Johnny-cake?"

He said: "I've outrun an old man, and an old woman, and a little boy, and two well-diggers, and two ditch-diggers, and a bear, and I can outrun you too-o-o!"

"Ye can, can ye?" snarled the wolf, "we'll see about that!" And he set into a gallop after Johnny-cake, who went on and on so fast that the wolf too saw there was no hope of overtaking him, and he too lay down to rest.

On went Johnny-cake, and by-and-by he came to a fox that lay quietly in a corner of the fence. The fox called out in a sharp voice, but without getting up: "Where ye going, Johnny-cake?"

He said: "I've outrun an old man, and an old woman, and a little boy, and two well-diggers, and two ditch-diggers, a bear, and a wolf, and I can outrun you too-o-o!"

The fox said: "I can't quite hear you, Johnny-cake. Won't you come a little closer?" turning his head a little to one side.

Johnny-cake stopped his race for the first time, and went a little closer, and called out in a very loud voice: *"I've outrun an old man, and an old woman, and a little boy, and two well-diggers, and two ditch-diggers, and a bear, and a wolf, and I can outrun you too-0-0."*

"Can't quite hear you; won't you come a *little* closer?" said the fox in a feeble voice, as he stretched out his neck towards Johnny-cake, and put one paw behind his ear.

Johnny-cake came up close, and leaning towards the fox screamed out: "I'VE OUTRUN AN OLD MAN, AND AN OLD WOMAN, AND A LITTLE BOY, AND TWO WELL-DIGGERS, AND TWO DITCH-DIGGERS, AND A BEAR, AND A WOLF, AND I CAN OUTRUN YOU TOO-O-O!"

"You can, can you?" yelped the fox, and

he snapped up the Johnny-cake in his sharp teeth in the twinkling of an eye.